"I'm Prince Robert!"

He knew in his bones it was true. He could feel his royal blood swirling around inside him.

"I was kidnapped the day I was born," he said. "I was just a baby, but I can remember now. The kidnappers hid me in a hospital. Mr. and Mrs. Redpost took me home from the hospital by mistake."

"You remember this?" asked Mrs. North. "From when you were one day old?"

"It's kind of a haze," Marvin admitted. "I don't remember exactly what the kidnappers looked like. One of them had a big black mustache."

More First Stepping Stone Books:

Dinosaurs Before Dark
(#1—The Magic Tree House series)
by Mary Pope Osborne

Junie B. Jones and the Stupid Smelly Bus
by Barbara Park

Coming in January 1993:

The Knight Before Dawn
(#2—The Magic Tree House series)
by Mary Pope Osborne

Junie B. Jones and a Little Monkey Business
by Barbara Park

Marvin Redpost: Why Pick on Me?
by Louis Sachar

MARVIN REDPOST: Kidnapped at Birth?

by Louis Sachar

illustrated by Neal Hughes

A FIRST STEPPING STONE BOOK

Random House 🏠 New York

Dedicated to Rebecca and Sam,
with special thanks to their parents

Text copyright © 1992 by Louis Sachar.
Illustrations copyright © 1992 by Neal Hughes.
All rights reserved under International and Pan-American
Copyright Conventions. Published in the United States by
Random House, Inc., and simultaneously in Canada by
Random House of Canada Limited, Toronto.

Library of Congress Cataloging-in-Publication Data
Sachar, Louis.   Marvin Redpost: Kidnapped at birth?
by Louis Sachar ; illustrated by Neal Hughes.   p.   cm.
"A First stepping stone book"—SUMMARY: Red-haired Marvin
is convinced that the reason he looks different from the rest of his
family is that he is really the lost prince of Shampoon.
ISBN 0-679-81946-0 (trade ed.) — ISBN 0-679-91946-5 (lib. bdg.)
[1. Redheads—Fiction.   2. Princes—Fiction.
3. Family life—Fiction.   4. Humorous stories.]
I. Hughes, Neal, ill.   II. Title.
PZ7.S1185Ki   1992   [Fic]—dc20   91-51105

Manufactured in the United States of America.
10 9 8 7 6 5 4 3 2 1

Contents

MARVIN REDPOST: Kidnapped at Birth?

1

Royal Blood

The End

Marvin Redpost put down his pencil. He was the first one done.

He took his report to Mrs. North.

Mrs. North looked at it. "I can't read this," she said.

He had to copy it over. "Neater this time, Marvin," said Mrs. North.

Marvin frowned.

He was in the third grade. His class had been learning cursive writing.

"It's because I'm left-handed," Marvin complained. "It's impossible to write neatly when you're left-handed. Everything is backwards."

"I'm left-handed," said Mrs. North.

"Oh," said Marvin.

"We're lucky to be left-handed," said Mrs. North. "It means we have royal blood."

She smiled at him.

"You'd write neater if you slowed down," she said. "It isn't a race."

He returned to his seat.

He picked up his pencil and wrote as fast as he could.

He had to write twice as fast this time, just to catch up with everyone else.

He had to write a report on something he read in *Current Events*. *Current Events* was a newspaper for children.

This is what Marvin wrote.

The King of Shampoon is looking for his lost son. The son's name is Prince Robert. Prince Robert was kidnapped the day he was born. That was nine years ago.

Prince Robert is nine years old. He has red hair and blue eyes. Unless he's dead.

The King is going all around the world looking for his lost son. He hopes he isn't dead. So do I. This week the King is in Washington, D.C.

<u>The End</u>

Marvin finished writing just as the bell rang for recess. He gave his report to Mrs.

North, then ran outside to play wall-ball.

Marvin was nine years old. He had red hair. He had blue eyes.

He lived in a small town, not too far from Washington, D.C.

2

You Can Do Anything!

Marvin had two best friends, Stuart Albright and Nick Tuffle.

After school they all went to Stuart's house.

"Put your dog outside," said Nick.

Nick was brave. He once rode his bike full speed down Suicide Hill. But he was afraid of Fluffy, Stuart's little white dog.

Marvin petted Fluffy.

"Careful, he's going to bite you," said Nick.

Fluffy growled at Nick.

"He's a good dog," said Marvin.

Fluffy licked Marvin's fingers.

Stuart put Fluffy outside.

"Where'd you get that stupid dog?" asked Nick.

"Fluffy's not stupid," said Stuart.

"He is too," said Nick. "He looks like a rat that ran through a cotton candy machine."

"We got him at the pound," said Stuart. "I picked him out myself."

"Well, you picked the wrong dog," said Nick.

"I did not!"

"Did too."

Marvin was afraid they'd get into a fight. Nick and Stuart were always getting into fights.

"I think my parents picked the wrong baby," Marvin said.

"Huh?" asked Nick.

"What?" said Stuart.

"At the hospital," said Marvin. "They took the wrong baby home. They're not really my parents."

He had been thinking about this all day. He didn't really believe it. He just wanted to keep his best friends from fighting.

"I was kidnapped the day I was born," said Marvin.

"You're Prince Robert!" exclaimed Stuart.

Stuart was smart. It sometimes amazed Marvin how quickly he caught on to things.

"Say what?" asked Nick.

"Marvin's parents are really the King and Queen of Shampoon," Stuart explained.

"Wait a second," said Nick. "Mr. and Mrs. Redpost? No way!"

"No," said Stuart. "Don't you remember what we read in *Current Events*? The Prince was kidnapped at birth."

"So?" said Nick.

"So Marvin is really Prince Robert," said Stuart.

"Say what?" said Nick.

"I have red hair and blue eyes," said Marvin. "Everyone else in my family has brown hair and brown eyes. And I'm left-handed. That means I have royal blood."

"Wait a second," said Nick. "If your parents are the King and Queen of Shampoon, then how did you end up in the hospital here?"

Marvin thought a moment. He hadn't figured that part out.

"Simple!" said Stuart. "The kidnappers had to hide the baby somewhere. Well, what better place to hide a baby than with a bunch of other babies in a hospital?"

"That's right!" said Marvin.

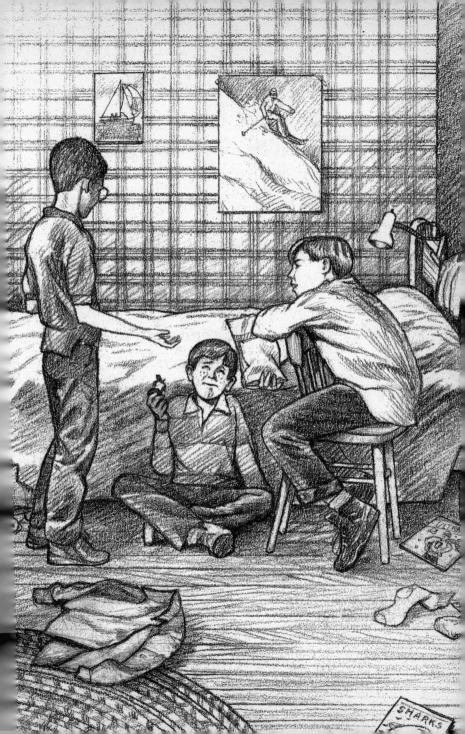

"Or," said Stuart, "maybe your parents didn't get you at the hospital. Maybe you're adopted. They just haven't told you."

"I bet you that's it!" said Nick. "The kidnappers left you in a garbage bin. Then a policeman found you and took you to an orphanage. And then Mr. and Mrs. Redpost adopted you."

"Or else," Stuart whispered, "Mr. and Mrs. Redpost might be the kidnappers."

"You'll get to live in a castle!" said Nick. "And you'll have a hundred servants. You'll never have to make your bed again."

Marvin shrugged.

"You'll have so much money," said Nick. "You could buy anything you want. You walk into a store. You see something you want. You just buy it. You could buy a car!"

Marvin laughed.

"I'm too young to drive," he said.

"Duh," said Nick. "No one's going to give the Prince a ticket! You can do anything. Darn, I wish I had red hair and blue eyes! You're so lucky, Marvin. Man, some people have all the luck!"

"I'm not lucky," Marvin reminded him. "I was unlucky to be kidnapped."

"We just have to figure out a way to tell the King," said Stuart. "And you can't let your parents know. If they're the kidnappers, they'll kill you for sure."

3

Marvin Sees the King

Marvin Redpost lived in a gray house. There was a fence around the house. The fence was all white except for one red post.

He slapped the red post as he walked through the gate.

He had an older brother, Jacob, who was eleven, and a younger sister, Linzy, who was four.

Jacob met him at the front door. "Watch out, Mar," he said. "Mom's mad."

"I'm not mad!" said their mother, coming up behind him.

She sounded mad.

"Go clean your room," she told Jacob.

"I already cleaned my room," said Jacob.

"Clean it again," she said. "Then help Linzy with hers."

Jacob was right. She was mad.

"And where have you been?" she asked Marvin.

"At Stuart's," he said.

"Grandma and Grandpa are coming over."

"I forgot."

"You should have called," said his mother. "You didn't tell me you were going to Stuart's house. I had no idea where you were!"

"I always go to Stuart's. Or Nick's," said Marvin.

"You are supposed to call," said his mother. "You could have been kidnapped, for all I knew!"

"Okay, okay. I'm sorry," said Marvin.

He went upstairs to his room. "I *was* kidnapped, for all you know," he muttered to himself.

He wondered if his mother would say that if she was really a kidnapper.

Probably not.

"I want you to do your homework!" his mother yelled up to him. "Before Grandma and Grandpa get here!"

"Okay, okay," Marvin muttered.

Marvin had a pet lizard named General Jackson. General Jackson lived in a glass cage next to Marvin's desk.

"She probably has no idea I'm Prince Robert," Marvin told the General. "If she did, she wouldn't yell at me. She'd serve me breakfast in bed every morning."

General Jackson stuck out his tongue.

For homework, Marvin had to practice his handwriting. He wrote as fast as he could.

"If I was a prince," he said, "I wouldn't have to do homework. A servant would do it for me."

He finished his homework, then walked downstairs. His grandparents still had not arrived.

His father was watching television in the den.

"Dad," said Marvin. "Was I adopted?"

"What? No, of course not."

"Would you tell me if I was?"

"Yes, but you weren't."

Marvin rubbed his chin. His father *seemed* to be telling the truth.

"What happened when I was born?" he asked.

"What?"

"Did anything unusual happen?"

His father looked away from the television. "Um, it seems there was something," he said. "I forget what it was. But it was a false alarm. You were fine." He turned back to the television.

"Did they take me away?" asked Marvin. "Or was I with Mom every single second?"

His father sighed. "No, you weren't with Mom every single second. Can we please talk about this later? I'm trying to watch the news."

"Well, when I came back," said Marvin, "did I look different?"

"*What?*"

"Okay," said Marvin. "Like three days after I was born. Did I look exactly the same as the day I was born?"

"I don't remember. Probably not. Babies change quickly."

"What did I look like when I was born?"

"You looked like a baby. All babies look pretty much the same. Now, please, Marvin. I want to watch this."

The doorbell rang.

Marvin heard his grandparents enter.

His father got up. "C'mon, Mar," he said.

But now Marvin was watching TV.

The King of Shampoon was on the news. The King had wavy red hair underneath his gold crown.

"I don't know if my son is alive or dead," said the King.

Except he spoke with a strange accent. So it sounded like "I don't know *eef* my son *ees* alive or dead."

The King's face filled the TV screen. He spoke. "Robert, if you're listening out there, please call me. Return to your rightful place

17

on the throne. We need you. Your kingdom awaits you."

Except it sounded like "*Vee* need you. Your kingdom *avaits* you."

The newsman came on. "If you think you may know someone who is Prince Robert, you should—"

The television shut off.

Mr. Redpost put down the remote-control switch. "Let's not keep Grandma and Grandpa waiting," he said.

Marvin's grandparents were making a big fuss over Linzy.

"You're so pretty, Linzy," said his grandmother. "You look more and more like your mother every day. And Jacob, you are the spitting image of your father."

"Who do I look like, Grandma?" asked Marvin.

His grandmother smiled at him. "You look like—" She stopped and thought a moment. "You look like both your parents," she said.

But Marvin knew she was just saying that. She really meant he didn't look like either of them.

He knew whom he looked like. He had just seen his face on television.

He looked like the King of Shampoon.

4

Marvin Redpost Is Dead

"Are you really the Lost Prince of Shampoon?" Judy Jasper asked Marvin as he walked into class.

"What?" asked Marvin. "Uh . . . I don't think so," he muttered.

"Nick said you were," said Melanie.

Travis and Kenny hurried over.

"Nick said you're the Lost Prince of Shampoon," said Kenny.

"Is that true?" asked Travis.

Before Marvin could answer, someone shoved him.

It was Clarence.

"You're not a prince!" said Clarence.

Clarence was the meanest kid in Marvin's class.

"I didn't say I was," said Marvin.

"You shouldn't push a prince, Clarence," said Judy. "He'll throw you in the dungeon."

"That's right," said Melanie.

"You're in big trouble, Clarence," said Travis.

"I'm not scared," said Clarence.

Nick put his arm around Marvin. "Hey, everybody," he said. "This is my best friend. Prince Robert."

Marvin took his seat. He wished Nick hadn't told everybody he was Prince Robert.

Casey Happleton sat down next to him. "Good morning, King Marvin," she said.

Marvin didn't answer.

"How are you today, King Marvin?" she asked.

Casey had a ponytail that stuck out of the side of her head. Not the back.

"Did you do your homework, King Marvin?" asked Casey.

"I'm not King Marvin!" Marvin snapped. "I'm Prince Robert!"

He said it.

It felt right. *I'm Prince Robert!* He had never liked the name Marvin.

Everyone was staring at him.

"Marvin?" asked Mrs. North.

He stood up. "My name's not Marvin," he said. "I'm Prince Robert, the Lost Prince of Shampoon."

He knew in his bones it was true. He could feel his royal blood swirling around inside him.

"I was kidnapped the day I was born," he

said. "I was just a baby, but I can remember now. The kidnappers hid me in a hospital. Mr. and Mrs. Redpost took me home from the hospital by mistake."

"You remember this?" asked Mrs. North. "From when you were one day old?"

"It's kind of a haze," Marvin admitted. "I don't remember exactly what the kidnappers looked like. One of them had a black mustache."

"Marvin has red hair," said Stuart. "Mr. and Mrs. Redpost have brown hair."

"How do you explain that?" asked Nick.

"Well, do any of your grandparents have red hair, Marvin?" asked Mrs. North.

Marvin thought a moment. "No. They all have gray hair. Or else they're bald. And I'm left-handed. You said that meant I have royal blood."

His teacher smiled. "Well, let me ask you a question, Marvin. Excuse me. I mean, Prince Robert. What ever happened to the real Marvin Redpost?"

"Huh?" said Marvin.

"Nine years ago Mr. and Mrs. Redpost had a baby. You say they took you home from the hospital by mistake. After the kidnappers hid you in the hospital. What happened to their real baby?"

"Some other parents took him home by mistake," suggested Nick.

"Then what about *their* baby?" asked Mrs. North.

"Other parents took him home," said Judy.

"So parents just keep taking home the wrong babies from this hospital?" asked Mrs. North.

"The real Marvin Redpost could have died," said Casey. "But then the people in the hospital discovered they had this extra baby. So they gave it to Mr. and Mrs. Redpost. And that way everybody was happy."

"Well, I suppose anything is possible," said Mrs. North.

"I watched the news last night," said Stuart. "The King of Shampoon was on. They gave a number to call. I wrote it down."

"Well, there you go," said Mrs. North. "All you have to do is call that number."

But at that moment, Marvin was feeling strangely sad.

He was thinking about what Casey Happleton said. The real Marvin Redpost was dead.

5

The Duchess of Bathwater

"So, what are you?" asked Clarence.

"Uh," said Marvin.

It was after school. He had just walked out of class with Nick and Stuart.

"He's a prince!" said Nick.

Marvin wished Nick hadn't said that.

Clarence glared at Marvin.

Marvin shrugged.

"I'm sorry I pushed you this morning," said Clarence.

"Huh?" said Marvin. "Oh, well, that's okay. I don't mind."

Clarence held out his hand.

Marvin shook it.

"Hah!" laughed Nick. "You're afraid Marvin'll throw you in the dungeon."

"I wouldn't do that," Marvin told Clarence. He wished Nick would quit saying things that could make Clarence mad.

Clarence looked at Marvin. "Do you want a quarter?" he asked.

Marvin shook his head.

Stuart elbowed him. "Take it, Marvin," he whispered.

Clarence pulled a quarter out of his pocket. "Here, you can have it."

"No, that's okay," said Marvin.

"Take it," said Clarence.

Marvin took it.

"Thanks," said Clarence.

"You're welcome," said Marvin.

Clarence walked away. Nick and Stuart cracked up.

Casey Happleton and Judy Jasper came out the door.

"Good-bye, Prince Marvin," said Casey.

"See you tomorrow, Prince," said Judy.

The two girls ran away, giggling.

Marvin looked at the quarter. He wished Clarence hadn't given it to him.

"A quarter is nothing to a prince," said Stuart. "Do you know how much your allowance is going to be?"

"A hundred dollars a week?" guessed Nick.

"More," said Stuart.

"A thousand?" asked Marvin.

Stuart shook his head. Then he said, "Your weight in gold."

Nick whistled.

"You should eat more," said Stuart. "The

more you weigh, the bigger your allowance."

"You could have three ice cream sundaes a day," said Nick.

"Four," said Stuart.

"Five," said Nick.

"Six!" said Marvin.

"C'mon," said Stuart. "Let's go to your house and call up your father."

"Why?" asked Marvin. His father worked at an office in Washington, D.C.

"The King of Shampoon," said Stuart.

"Oh, my *father*!" said Marvin.

"Duh," said Nick.

They went to Marvin's house. He tapped the red post as he walked through the gate.

They went straight to the phone in the kitchen. Stuart gave Marvin the number to call.

Marvin looked at the phone.

"Don't you want to call him?" asked Stuart.

"Sure, I do," said Marvin.

He wasn't sure.

"Well, do it," said Nick.

"I will," Marvin said. "Don't rush me." He picked up the phone.

"What are you going to say?" asked Nick.

Marvin took a deep breath, then dialed the number.

"Are you going to call him *Dad*?" asked Nick.

A woman answered the phone. "How may I direct your call, please?" she asked.

"I would like to speak to His Royal Highness, the King of Shampoon, please," said Marvin.

"Oh, that's good," said Nick.

"I'm sorry, the King isn't here. May I help you?" said the woman.

"It's me!" exclaimed Marvin. "I'm the King's son. The one he's looking for."

"And your name?"

"My name?" Marvin smiled at Nick and Stuart. "Prince Robert."

The woman laughed. "That may very well be," she said. "However, we've received lots of calls. Do you go by a different name?"

"Oh," said Marvin. "Marvin Redpost."

"And when can you come in for your test?"

"My test?"

"Yes, a blood test."

"Oh," said Marvin. "I was afraid I'd have to know the capital of Shampoon, or stuff like that."

The woman laughed. "No, it's not that kind of test," she said.

Marvin liked the way the woman laughed. It sounded almost as if she was singing.

"How about eleven o'clock tomorrow?" she asked.

"I have school," said Marvin.

"Four-thirty?" asked the woman.

"Okay," said Marvin.

She told him where to go for the test. It was at the Watergate Hotel in Washington, D.C. Fifth floor.

"Excuse me. Are you my mother?" asked Marvin.

"What?"

"The Queen?" asked Marvin.

She laughed again. "No," she said. "I'm just—" She stopped. "I'm Lady Jennifer, Duchess of Bathwater."

"Oh," said Marvin. "Well, it was very nice talking to you, Lady Jennifer."

"It was nice talking to you, Marvin. I hope you really are Prince Robert. I like you."

Marvin hung up the phone. "Tomorrow at 4:30," he told his two best friends. "Now all I have to do is get my mom to take me there."

6

A New Car
for Mrs. Redpost

Marvin was sitting at the dinner table. Mrs. Redpost had made chicken tacos. His favorite.

He hoped she wasn't really a kidnapper. Then he'd have to lock her in the dungeon.

"Mr. and Mrs. Redpost," he said. "I have something important to tell you."

Mr. Redpost crunched into a taco. The juice ran down his sleeve.

"Mr. and Mrs. Redpost?" asked Mrs. Redpost.

"Linzy. Jake. You need to hear this too," said Marvin.

He took a breath. He wasn't quite sure how to say it.

"Well?" said Jacob.

"Marvin Redpost is dead," said Marvin.

Jacob laughed.

Mr. and Mrs. Redpost stared at him.

"And when did this happen?" asked Mr. Redpost.

"About nine years ago," said Marvin.

"Well, I must say," Mrs. Redpost noted, "you are looking quite well, considering."

Then she and Mr. Redpost cracked up.

Linzy burst into tears. "I love you, Marvin," she sobbed. "Don't be dead."

"Don't cry, Linzy," said Marvin. "*I'm* not dead. Marvin Redpost is dead. I'm not Marvin Redpost."

Linzy kept crying.

"You're not?" asked Mr. Redpost.

"No," said Marvin. He turned to his former mother. "Sorry, Mom. I mean, Mrs. Redpost. I know this comes as a great shock to you."

"Well, it certainly is a surprise," she replied.

"Who are you?" asked Jacob.

Marvin took a deep breath. "My name is

Prince Robert. I'm the Lost Prince of
Shampoon."

"Oh, I heard about him!" exclaimed Jacob.
"The King of Shampoon is in Washington
looking for his lost son!" He turned to Marvin.
"You're him? Neat!"

"I think so," said Marvin.

Marvin explained the whole thing to his family. How the kidnappers hid the baby prince in the hospital where Marvin Redpost was born. Then Marvin Redpost died, but they had an extra baby lying around, so they gave it to Mr. and Mrs. Redpost.

"Well, it all sounds very logical," Mr. Redpost agreed.

Linzy stopped crying, but her lower lip still trembled.

Marvin felt sorry for her. It is always hardest on the children.

"I've got red hair and blue eyes," Marvin said. "Everyone else in this family has brown hair and brown eyes."

"So what do you plan to do about this?" asked Mrs. Redpost.

"Stuart got the phone number from the news," said Marvin. "I called it. I spoke to Lady

Jennifer, Duchess of Bathwater."

Marvin stopped. Now came the hard part.

"I'm supposed to go to the Watergate Hotel tomorrow at 4:30. For a blood test. Can you please take me there, Mrs. Redpost?"

She looked at him.

"I know it's asking a lot," said Marvin. "Especially since you're not my mother. But I'm sure the King would be very grateful. He'll probably pay for the gas. I bet he'd even buy you a new car."

"I'll be happy to," said Mrs. Redpost.

"Thank you," said Marvin.

"I'm going to miss you, Marvin," said Mrs. Redpost.

7
They're All Exactly Like You!

The next afternoon Marvin sat in his room, waiting to go. He wondered what he should take. Maybe he should pack a suitcase.

"Wait a second," he said. "It's not like I can't come back here."

Prince Robert could do anything!

He could come back later for all his junk. Or better yet, send a servant for it.

"Do you want to live in a castle, General?" he asked his lizard.

General Jackson stuck out his tongue.

Jacob came in. "I just thought of something, Mar," he said. "Maybe Mom and Dad are really the kidnappers."

"I thought about that too," said Marvin. "But then she wouldn't take me for the blood test. It'd be too risky."

"Unless. . . ." said Jacob.

"What?"

"Unless she's not really going to take you."

"What do you mean?"

"No, never mind," said Jacob. "If she killed you, she'd have to kill me and Linzy too. She wouldn't do that."

"Probably not," Marvin agreed. "Not Linzy, anyway."

"Marvin!" shouted Linzy from the bottom of the stairs. "Time to go!"

They got in the car.

Jacob and Linzy were going along. They

planned to meet Mr. Redpost for dinner in the city.

"You're welcome to come to dinner too, Prince," said Mrs. Redpost. "If you're not too busy."

"Thank you," replied Marvin. "But I imagine I'll have a lot to do."

He knew Mr. and Mrs. Redpost didn't believe he was Prince Robert. He saw the way they had smiled at each other when he told them about it.

They probably thought it was just some kid-thing he was doing.

That was okay. Just so long as Mrs. Redpost was taking him to the Watergate Hotel. It didn't matter what she thought.

"You won't play baseball anymore," said Jacob. "You'll have to learn how to play polo."

"I can play polo," said Linzy.

"You can not," said Jacob.

"I can too," said Linzy. "Marco."

"Polo," said Marvin.

"Marco," said Linzy.

"Polo," said Marvin.

Marvin played "polo" with Linzy all the way to the hotel. It was a stupid game, but he didn't mind.

He was going to miss playing stupid games with Linzy.

Mrs. Redpost parked the car at the Watergate Hotel. They walked across the parking lot and into the lobby.

"No! I don't want to!" a boy shouted. He had red hair.

The boy's mother was dragging him across the lobby.

"Come on!" she yelled.

The boy was crying.

"We'll be rich," said the mother.

"But I'm not Prince Robert!" the boy cried.

"Shut up, Arnold!" said his mother. "Someone might hear you." She pulled him into the elevator.

Marvin and the Redposts got into the elevator too.

The woman looked at Marvin. "Who do you think *you* are?" she asked in a nasty voice.

Marvin was too afraid to answer.

"You are speaking to Prince Robert," said Mrs. Redpost, sticking up for him.

Marvin smiled at his former mother. Mrs. Redpost patted his head.

"I'm not that stupid prince," said the other boy. "I don't even have red hair. My mother made me dye it."

"Shut up, Arnold," said the nasty woman.

They got off the elevator and walked to

the suite at the end of the hall. The door was open.

Linzy laughed. "They're all exactly like you, Marvin!"

Marvin entered the room. He had never seen so many red-haired boys in all his life.

8

Number 812

A man in a white coat stepped out from behind a door. "Number seven sixty-seven," he called.

A red-haired boy followed him back through the door.

"You sure you'll be okay?" asked Mrs. Redpost.

Marvin nodded.

"Okay. We'll be back in about an hour." She kissed Marvin.

Marvin watched the Redposts leave. They were a nice family.

There was a line of red-haired boys going up to a desk. Marvin got on the end of the line.

"We were here first!" said the nasty woman from the elevator. She cut in line in front of Marvin, dragging her son with her.

Marvin let them in. It didn't matter who was first. There was only one Prince Robert.

The man in the white coat came back out. "Seven sixty-eight," he called.

Another red-haired boy followed him through the door.

"When you're Prince Robert, you can do anything!" the nasty woman told her son. "Just sit on your throne all day, eat candy, and boss people around."

The man in the white coat came out several more times.

"Seven sixty-nine."

"Seven seventy."

"Seven seventy-one."

Each time another red-haired boy followed him through the door.

Marvin was almost to the front of the line.

The woman behind the desk was wearing big gold earrings. As Marvin got closer he noticed that one earring was shaped like a dog. The other was a cat.

"Next," said the lady with the earrings.

The nasty woman and Arnold stepped to the front of the line.

"Your name?" muttered the earring lady. She seemed tired and bored.

"Arnold Miller," answered the nasty woman.

"Eight eleven," said the earring lady. She handed Arnold a slip of paper. "Next."

"Your name?"

"Marvin Redpost."

The earring lady looked up, and her face turned bright. "Oh, hi, Marvin!"

Marvin looked at her. "Hi," he said, unsure.

"I'm Jennifer," said the earring lady.

"Oh, hi!" said Marvin. "I mean—I am delighted to make your acquaintance, Lady Jennifer, Duchess of Bathwater." He bowed.

Jennifer laughed.

It was that same musical laugh he heard over the telephone.

"I'm not really a duchess," she said. "I just made that up. This is a part-time job."

"Oh," said Marvin.

"I wouldn't want to be a duchess anyway," said Jennifer. "It sounds so *stuffy* and *boring*. All that—" She stopped, then said, "I guess you want to be a prince, and that's okay. But it's not for me."

She wrinkled her nose.

Marvin shrugged. "I like your earrings," he said.

Jennifer laughed. "Thank you, Marvin. Well, good luck."

She gave him number **812**.

He thanked her.

"You're welcome," said Jennifer. "You know what I like about you, Marvin?" she asked.

"You're polite. No one else has said *thank you* to me all day."

"What happens when they call your number?" he asked her.

"You just go back for a blood test. To find out your blood type. The King and Queen have blood type *O negative.* So that means Prince Robert has to have blood type *O negative* too. It's pretty rare. Most people are type *A* or *B.* And almost everyone is positive, not negative."

"So then what happens?" asked Marvin.

"Well, if you're *A* or *B,* you're sent home. If you're *O negative,* you do a second blood test. It's called an HLA test. It's a lot more complicated. But it will tell for certain if you're Prince Robert."

"So they haven't found Prince Robert yet?" asked Marvin.

"No." She shrugged. "Otherwise we wouldn't be here. I don't think they'll ever find him. The odds are one in a million."

Marvin found it all a little confusing.

"Just hope your blood type is *O negative,*" said Jennifer. "That's the first step."

9

Blood Test

Marvin waited with all the other red-haired boys. He thought about what Linzy had said. "They're all exactly like you, Marvin!"

He knew that wasn't true. He was different. Special. He was the one and only Prince Robert.

He looked at his slip of paper.

812

He noticed one of the other boys had a yellow number. Everyone else's was black, like his.

"Eight eleven," called the man in the white coat.

Marvin watched the nasty woman drag Arnold through the door.

"I don't want to get a shot!" Arnold screamed.

A short while later the man returned. "Eight twelve."

Marvin stood up. Jennifer smiled and waved to him.

He walked through the door.

Marvin watched the man unwrap a new needle. Then he looked away.

If he didn't watch, it didn't hurt.

The man stuck the needle into Marvin's arm.

Once it was in, it was okay to look. Marvin watched his blood flow out of his arm and

slowly fill the tube. It felt weird watching his own blood.

"Thank you," Marvin said when the man was through.

"What?" asked the man. "Oh. You're welcome."

Marvin took his tube of blood through another door to the lab. He saw his number, 812, typed on the outside of the tube.

He gave the tube to a woman with glasses, then waited while she examined his blood.

She returned a short time later and handed him a new slip of paper. On it was written:

812
O negative

Royal blood!

10

One in a Million

"You'll have to take another blood test," said the woman with glasses. "You'll need to give a lot more blood this time."

"Why didn't they just take more blood the first time?" asked Marvin.

"It's a lot easier this way," the woman explained. "We see about a thousand kids a day. Fewer than fifty are *O negative*. So this way we only have to do about fifty HLA tests instead of a thousand."

She told Marvin to go back to the front

desk and get a new number. A yellow number, this time.

He walked back out to the main room. It was still full of red-haired boys. *They're all exactly like you, Marvin!* Linzy had said.

Now, more than ever, he knew that wasn't true. The proof was in his hand.

He got on line to get a new number from Jennifer. A yellow number.

"Eight thirty-nine," called the man in the white coat.

The nasty woman was leaving with her son.

"Can't you ever do anything right!" she shouted.

"I'm sorry. I'm sorry," said Arnold. "I told you I wasn't a prince."

"Shut up and get in the elevator," said the nasty woman.

Marvin thought about Mrs. Redpost. He

was glad she wasn't like that woman.

He remembered the time she tried to teach him to ice-skate. She was worse than he was. They both kept falling down. It was funny. But they both learned to ice-skate—sort of.

Marvin smiled as he remembered. They had hot chocolate afterward.

He thought about Jacob and Linzy. He thought about the house, with the red post in front.

Mr. Redpost painted that post once a year.

He looked at the slip of paper in his hand.

812

O negative

Then he suddenly remembered something. The King of Shampoon spoke with a weird accent! Marvin didn't talk like that. So that meant he couldn't be Prince Robert!

"Marvin, you're back!" said Jennifer. "So are you *O negative*?" she asked eagerly.

"Uh—" said Marvin. He stuffed the slip of paper into his pocket. "No," he said. "I just wanted to say good-bye."

Jennifer smiled at him. "I'm glad you stopped by," she said. She held her hand out across the desk. "Well, good-bye Marvin. I mean—I was delighted to make your acquaintance . . . *Prince Charming*."

Marvin blushed as he shook her hand.

His mother returned with Linzy and Jacob.

"Hi, Mom," he greeted her.

"Mom?" she asked. "Does this mean—?"

"Yes," said Marvin. "Marvin Redpost isn't dead."

"I'm sorry," said his mother.

"Yay!" shouted Linzy.

He went out to dinner with his family.

A week later the King of Shampoon left Washington, D.C., still looking for his lost son.

Marvin felt sorry for him.

He thought about all the red-haired boys in the hotel room.

But he was different. Special. He was the one and only Marvin Redpost.

Besides, he probably wasn't Prince Robert anyway. The odds were one in a million.

"I won," Clarence declared.

"You did not," said Marvin. "The ball was over the line."

"You're crazy," said Clarence.

"I saw it," said Marvin.

"You did not," said Clarence. "You weren't even watching. You were picking your nose!"

Several of the kids on line laughed.

"It was over the line," said Marvin.

"Go pick your nose," said Clarence.

The kids on line laughed again, even Nick.

From *Marvin Redpost: Why Pick on Me?*
by Louis Sachar

About the Author

Louis Sachar does not have red hair or royal blood. However, he *is* known for his incredibly funny books, including *There's a Boy in the Girls' Bathroom* (winner of sixteen children's choice awards). When asked if he remembers being in third grade, Louis admits that it's "kind of a haze." But he adds, "When I start writing, it all comes back to me."

Louis Sachar (rhymes with cracker) lives in Austin, Texas, with his wife, Carla, and their daughter, Sherre.